Happy Birthday!

Adapted by Annie Auerbach

ISBN 978-1-338-89192-8

 10 9 8 7 6 5 4 3 2 1
Printed in the U.S.A.

23 24 25 26 27
40

Licensed by:

This edition first printing 2023
Book design by Mercedes Padró
www.peppapig.com

SCHOLASTIC INC.

Today is Peppa's birthday. Peppa wakes up with a snort. She is too excited to stay in bed!

"George, wake up!" says
Peppa. "It's my birthday. I'm
going to have a party, and
Daddy's doing a magic show!"

Peppa and George rush into Mummy and Daddy Pig's bedroom.

"Wake up! It's my birthday!" shouts Peppa.
Daddy Pig yawns and looks at the clock.
"It's five o'clock in the morning!" he says.

"Yes," says Peppa. "See how much time has passed already!" Mummy Pig chuckles. "Okay, let's get your birthday started." "Yippee!" cheers Peppa.

Downstairs in the kitchen, Mummy and Daddy Pig set out bowls of Peppa's favorite cereal for a birthday breakfast.

Before they eat, George gives Peppa her present.
"Happy birthday, Peppa!" everyone says.

"Ooh!" says Peppa. She shakes
the box. "What is it?" she asks.
Peppa unwraps the present.

"A doll's dress!" she exclaims.
"I can put it on Teddy! Thank
you, everyone!"
"You're welcome, Peppa," says
Daddy Pig.

Daddy Pig is very excited to be the magician for Peppa's party. "You will introduce me as the Amazing Mysterio," he tells Peppa.

Peppa is not so sure she can remember that. But she can't wait for her party!

A little while later, the doorbell rings.
"My friends are here!" says Peppa.
"Hello, everyone!"

"Hello, Peppa! Happy birthday!"
say her friends.

It is time for the magic show! Peppa must introduce Daddy Pig to her friends.

"Ladies and gentlemen," begins Peppa. But she can't remember what to say next!

"Um . . ." she says. "It's . . .
Magic Daddy!"
"Hooray!" everyone shouts
and claps.

Daddy begins his first magic trick.
"Abracadabra!" he says. Then he pulls
something special out of his top hat.
"Wow!" says Peppa. "It's Teddy!"

Peppa and her friends clap.
Daddy Pig takes a bow.

For Daddy Pig's next trick, Suzy Sheep will
be his helper. Daddy Pig gives Suzy three
colorful balls. With his back turned, he is
going to guess which ball she chooses.

"Abracadabra!" says Daddy Pig. He guesses
that Suzy is holding the yellow ball.

"No," says Suzy.
Daddy Pig guesses the blue ball.
"No," says Suzy.
Daddy Pig guesses the red ball.
That's the one!

"Silly Magic Daddy," Peppa says.
"You said all three colors!"
"Hush, Peppa," whispers Daddy Pig.
"Don't tell anyone!"

But everyone hears them,
and everyone giggles.

"Would you like to see one more trick?" Daddy Pig asks the children. "Yes, please!" everyone says. Daddy Pig tells them to close their eyes. "Now say the magic word: Abracadabra!"

"Abracadabra!" everyone shouts.
"Now open your eyes," says Daddy Pig.
Mummy Pig has brought out Peppa's
birthday cake!

Now all Peppa has to do is make a wish and blow out the candles! "This was my favorite magic trick," Peppa says. "And this is my best birthday ever!"

Punch out this birthday card along the perforation. Then fold it in half and share it with a friend on their birthday!

Happy Birthday!

On your special day,
Peppa Pig would like to say . . .

Happy Birthday!